INANIMATES

THE VEILED WORLD SERIES (Written as Jo Anderton)

Debris

Suited

Guardian

COLLECTIONS

The Bone Chime Song and Other Stories

FOR CHILDREN

The Flying Optometrist (illustrated by Karen Erasmus)

INANIMATES

Tales of Everyday Fear

JOANNE ANDERTON

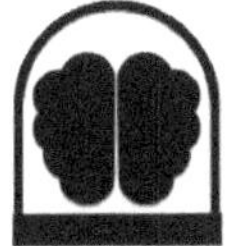

Brain Jar Press
PO Box 6687
Upper Mt Gravatt, QLD, 4122
Australia
www.BrainJarPress.com

Cover design by Peter Ball
Cover Image: Skull shapes smoke from burned candle, Tithi Luadthong/Shutterstock

ISBN: 978-1-922479-12-9 (print); 978-1-922479-13-6 (ebook)

Contents

Preface

Short story collections can mess with our heads. Sometimes, we write them with purpose, beginning with a theme in mind, a thread that binds them all together. Other times – as is the case with this one – we gather up reprints, stories that have already been out in the world. They're older, those stories, world-weary perhaps. It's been a while since we last checked in on them. They were written independently of each other, over the span of years. Some went on to greater things, to awards or reviews or best-ofs. Some, maybe, never got the recognition we thought they deserved. Either way, they've come home now, and so we look at them with fresh eyes. See things we didn't notice, the first time around.

And this is where they start messing with us. Because even though we wrote them, we never really knew them. Stories have a life of their own, and they have things to teach us. The words we write expose parts of ourselves… even if we'd rather they didn't. They uncover truths. Reveal fears.

Inanimates: Tales of everyday fear is a short collection of horror and dark fiction, seven stories that were not created together, and yet fit so nicely it's like they were always meant to be. Written over several years, published in different markets, formats, and countries, they track an unspoken fear of mine that I'd never really confronted, until now.

Of the darkness that lingers in the everyday.

A common feeling of threat from the 'normal' world weaves its way through the collection, and the first and last stories – *The Sea at Night* and *High Density* – explore it in urban and particularly *Sydney* ways. Maroubra beach, my local for so long, changes in *The Sea at Night* from a site of sunshine and surf to a place of darkness, of emptiness and endless hunger. In *High Density*, the modernisation and gentrification of my once-working class suburb becomes a literal life and death struggle against the way progress changes us, houses and humans both.

The seaside cliffs of Coogee and Clovelly provided the setting and inspiration for *Little Ghost Boy*, but this story, along with *Cold Beneath the Bougainvillea*, explores fear of connection to the creatures in our lives. Anyone who knows me – or has had even the briefest conversation with me, or so much as glanced at my socials – knows I'm a pet person. But for all the love animals bring, they also bring grief, because the closer we get to anyone – or anything – the keener we feel the loss when they leave. Which everything inevitably does.

Simulation Theory takes the depth of this relationship between owner and pet, human and companion, to a whole other level, and adds a dash of science fiction to spice up all the horror. It also challenges the line between living thing and inanimate object. Can we really pretend to have no bond with the 'things' in our lives? The remaining stories, *Mirror Dirt* and *Thread Embrace*, probe the unsettling affection we feel for our belongings. Who hasn't imagined that a beautiful object, a cherished possession, has a personality of its own?

And if they do, then what to we owe them? And what do they think of us?

The stories in *Inanimates: Tales of everyday fear* showed me a part of myself that I didn't know existed, an anxiety about the so-called real world and the way it steals into me – and threatens to take over. I hope, in reading these stories, you find a part of yourself as well. That, like a mirror stained with creeping dirt, they reflect the hidden, everyday fears that lurk beneath your surface.

Because we need to see the darkness, acknowledge it, if we're going to survive it. And that's what horror is for.

The Sea at Night

Joe dug his bare feet into the sand on Maroubra beach as night fell. The dark sea reached forward to wash over his skin and suck at the dirty hems of his pants. A glance over his shoulder showed the beach was emptying. The odd preoccupied couple and fish-and-chips-eating family remained on the steps behind him, but didn't venture onto the sand. Even further back the streetlights flickered on and seemed to congregate, with all the movement and the noise, at the Maroubra Bay Hotel on the corner.

Joe knelt so the tide dampened his knees, and began to dig. He did so with small, practiced movements, filtering sand through his fingers, feeling rather than seeing. He'd spent every evening for years doing this, searching in the warm waves for the parts of him the demon had taken away. He'd come close a couple of times: he'd caught the tips of his own youthful fingers bobbing in the foam, and he'd even found strips of the suit he'd bought for the wedding that never happened, teasing and trailing like seaweed with the tide.

But he'd never found enough to rebuild what the demon

had destroyed. So he kept digging. And he was so preoccupied that he didn't hear footsteps on the sand until their owner appeared by his side.

'That's a strange activity, isn't it, for this time of day?'

Joe didn't stop, merely glanced up. The man who addressed him was little more than a thin silhouette in a suit against the streetlights, hands clasped behind him and bent forward from the waist. Joe turned back to his digging.

'And for a fully dressed man, now that I think of it.'

Joe gave a little shrug and shuffled crab like along the water's edge. 'Not fully dressed,' he mumbled, 'got no shoes.'

'Hmm, no I suppose you don't.' The man appeared to follow him, but so softly he didn't make a sound. 'But that doesn't make it any less strange.'

Joe sighed, sat back on his sand-encrusted heels and wiped his hands on the front of his pants. 'You going to leave me alone, or what?' He stood with a creak and a grunt, and turned his scowl on the man. One look at the fresh scars on Joe's face, his reeking mess of matted hair, and the three layers of soiled shirts he was wearing, and surely this bloke would leave him alone.

But this man wasn't normal either. He was pale, too pale for any skin that'd seen the sun. His cheeks were sunken and his eyes large, like a starving child, lips thin and white. His suit was old, moth-eaten in patches and so heavy with dust it floated on the sea breeze, a soft shower glittering in the light from the street.

Caught off-guard, Joe took a hesitant step back. The tall man seemed to flicker, then. One moment he was standing there, hands behind his back and gaunt face curious, and the next he folded in on himself and reappeared, a step closer. Like a bloody piece of paper. He left no footprints, and sounded like the beating of wings.

Joe blinked, shook his head. 'Sorry, mate,' he said. 'I didn't realise you were like me.'

The man lifted eyebrows so thin they could have been drawn onto his forehead. 'Oh? And what are we?'

'Dark. Dirty. Different.' That sounded pretty bad, so Joe tried again. 'We're like the sea at night. Doesn't matter how many lights this city turns on we're always there, the dark tide, lapping at its feet, eating away at its precious security.' Well, maybe his nonsensical rambling would get rid of the guy anyway. 'Sydney doesn't like the parts of it that aren't bright and clean and happy, but that's what we are. So we're like the sea, but at night...' He stuttered off into silence.

After a moment the man unclasped his hands and held one out. 'My name is Gideon,' he said. 'At this point in time, anyway.' His nails were very short and very clean, and his hand so thin it was almost bones.

Joe lifted a hand but hesitated. His nails were long and currently clogged with sand.

'Oh please,' Gideon said, 'you don't have to worry about that with me.'

They shook. Gideon was cold but his grip strong. 'Joseph,' Joe said.

Gideon nodded, expression thoughtful. 'I'd like to get to know you better, Joe. Can I buy you a beer?' He motioned to the pub.

Joe shook his head. Even if the Hotel security let him inside – with his dirty clothes and his weeping scars and his overall stench – Joe didn't belong in that bright world, with all those people. And anyway, he had to keep digging.

'Oh come on,' Gideon said. He folded and fluttered away from the water's edge, towards the street, and despite himself Joe was drawn to follow. 'You won't find what you're looking for here, anyway. What you have lost cannot be recovered from the sand.'

The steps were empty, now, cluttered only with loose sand tossed there by the wind. The night wrapped Gideon in a cloak that reached out, in shapes like quivering wings, to douse the nearby streetlights one by one. He led Joe through the small park and across the road. All around them, life and movement faded. The old stoners sitting outside the kebab shop took their food inside; the fish and chips closed its doors, despite the oil and the heat; even the bus stop and the pub's outdoor courtyard cleared.

'It's better this way,' Gideon said, his voice as deep as the sea. 'Don't you agree?'

Two steps inside the Maroubra Bay Hotel and security stopped them. The usual large men without expressions. 'This is the point where I turn around and leave,' Joe muttered.

One of the security guards nodded to him. 'Good idea, mate.' He pointed to Gideon. 'You can stay, but your friend needs a bath before we let him in here.'

But Gideon said, 'No, he has as much right to a beer as the rest of you.' As he spoke the shadows that draped across his shoulders spread. The lights along the gaudily striped walls flickered and snapped off, all at once. The wide TV screens that streamed surfing and the ever-present sun sizzled into curtains of white noise. Only the lights behind the bar remained, casting the surreal colours and shapes of bottles of alcohol across the room.

'Come on,' Gideon tugged Joe forward. 'You need a beer.'

One of the guards tried to stop them. Gideon brushed him aside like he was swatting a fly, and sent him crashing through furniture to collapse against a far wall. The pub's patrons fled as Gideon approached the bar, leaving dust like a tide-line in his wake.

The barman remained, looking ghoulish in the alcoholic light, though his hands shook as he pulled them each a schooner. Gideon hadn't asked the type of beer he wanted, but Joe decided not to press the issue.

'You may leave now.' Gideon waved his hand and feathers rustled in the movement. The barman fled. Probably a good idea.

Gideon lifted the beer to his lips, smiled thinly against the glass. 'Go on,' he said. 'I know it has been years since you drank anything not wrapped in a brown paper bag.' His pale skin, stretched so tightly across his skull, turned to a decaying yellow in the light. His eyes were nothing but black hollows and everything but his head and hands was lost in shadow.

Joe sipped his beer. Gideon pretended to drink: he touched the amber liquid to his lips but didn't so much as open his mouth. Add that to the darkness and the mysterious powers and superhuman strength, and it didn't take much to work out.

'So—' Joe was careful to place a coaster beneath his dripping glass '—are you a demon too?'

Something like moonlight flashed in the holes that were Gideon's eyes, then he lowered his beer and pushed it across the bar. 'Here, you might as well have mine too. I'm hardly going to drink it, now am I?' When he spoke, his mouth was strange, lips tense and teeth never showing, yet Joe had no trouble understanding him.

Joe shrugged, tossed back his, and took the demon's glass. Did it really matter where the beer came from, as long as it was cold? 'I don't know why you've chosen me. I don't have much left to take, you know. Another of your kind got to me first.'

Gideon wrinkled his nose in a surprisingly genteel expression of disgust. 'I would hardly call the demon that got you one of my kind. And you have plenty left, for someone like me.' He leaned forward, face close to Joe's neck and breathed in deeply. 'But you surprised me, back there on the sand. I thought I knew men like you.' He leaned back. 'But you had *remarkable* things to say. So take the opportunity, Joe my boy, and enjoy your beer.'

That he could do. So, Gideon was a demon. There was no point panicking about it. Not now.

'Tell me about the sea.'

Joe shifted, uncomfortable on the barstool. 'The sea?'

'I liked it, what you said. Lapping away at the city's security. You said you felt like that, Joe. And that we were the same. But why would you say that? Was that the demon talking?'

Joe frowned, took a good long drink. Gideon's eyes widened and he snatched the empty glass, flickered around behind the bar and filled it again. A strange sight, all that growing, reaching shadow pouring drinks.

This was more beer in one sitting than he'd had for years. Despite the yeasty sickness gathering in his stomach, Joe was enjoying it. For the first time in almost as many years he was drinking in the company of... well, if not friends then at least with someone other than himself.

'The demon isn't here to do any talking,' Joe answered, after a moment's thought. 'It tore out the best parts of me and left me like this. Scarred. Dirty. Lapping at the edges of my old life like the sea, at night.'

A curious twitch of his eyebrows. 'How'd it happen?' Gideon even collected a cloth and wiped the bar as he spoke. It made Joe smile. 'Warm summer day, of course. When the tide was turning – going in or out, it never matters – and the rips were strong. Too strong, much stronger than you realised. Were you surfing?'

Joe shook his head. 'Just swimming. Was never any good on a board.'

'And the rip got you. Took you far.'

Why was he asking, if he already knew? 'Did what I was told, waved and shouted at those bloody flags till I was hoarse. But the rip had hold of me, carried me away from the beach. The land disappeared, the sand fell away underneath and there was nothing but me, and the sea and the hard sky like its reflection.'

'Ah.' Gideon closed his eyes. 'The hard sky like its reflection. Were you a poet, Joe, before the demon took you?'

He snorted beer through his nose at that. 'Hardly, mate. Plumber, and I reckon it pays better.' He glanced around, searching for food. Too much bloody beer too quickly.

'I'm sure it does. And yet, I have not seen the hard blue sky for, well, for a long time, and you paint it so beautifully.' Gideon paused, frowned. 'What is it?'

'Seen anything to nibble on?'

A packet of salt and vinegar chips fluttered through darkness and wings to land on the bar before him.

'Perfect.' Joe tore them open and offered them to Gideon first, out of courtesy, though he knew the demon wouldn't accept. 'Cheers.'

'And then?' Gideon whispered.

'Reckon you know.'

'Tell me.'

Joe shrugged, even though his stomach was rolling at the memory, and took a moment to chew a chip, sharp and biting against his tongue. 'And then there was the demon. Thought it was my own reflection, first, wavering before me on the mirror of the sea. Looked like me, almost like me. Me if I wasn't terrified but, well, enjoying myself. Turned out those hands weren't mine, and they reached out of the water and straight into my chest. Took... Touched... Well, you know. Next thing I was dumped, water in my mouth and sand in everything. And ever since I dragged myself out of that water, that bright and terrible clear water, nothing's been the same.'

'Because the demon took the best of you.'

'Yep.' Another swig, damn the nausea. 'Ruined my life. Lost my job, lost my fiancé, lost my house. And ended up like this.'

'It ruined your life?' Was that disappointment on Gideon's face? 'Do you hate what the demon has made of you?'

'Of course I do.' He frowned. 'What kind of question is that?'

'The way you spoke about the darkness and sea – with such beauty, Joe the Plumber – I thought you might be different from the rest. Maybe you belong in the darkness.' Gideon ran a hand over his bony face. 'But you don't, not really. You want to return to the way things used to be, before the demon came. When you belonged to that bright city and its people.'

'Yep – I had a life then, you know. So I've got to keep digging. To find the me it took.' Joe tried to stand, teetered on the edge of the stool and fell back into Gideon's waiting hands. Damn he could flicker about so fast. 'Thanks for the beer. Nice of you, really was.'

'Careful,' Gideon said. Joe glanced back and caught the tips of two teeth, long and far too sharp, peeking out of the demon's taut lips. 'Not so fast.' He growled beneath those words, an inhuman noise rumbling from deep within.

'Cheers.' Joe patted what should have been a shoulder, but something large and covered in fur – or was it feathers? – twitched and rolled beneath his hand. 'You're a mate. A demon, but a mate.'

Gideon laughed, and great fangs arched like moonlit scythes out of his maw. A reek like the grave wafted over Joe's face. Gideon steadied him, turned him and held his shoulders so their faces were close. Joe homeless and filthy and ever-scarred; Gideon terrible and dark, lit in places only by the moon.

'Oh Joe, I am not. I *am* the dark you hate so much, so I can't be your mate, don't you see? I thought you might be different, but who would want to be one of us if they had a choice? It's lonely in the sea at night, isn't it?' He leaned in and Joe felt pressure, sharp and strange, against the scabs on his neck. Gideon hugged him tightly, and all Joe's body was cold, everything like ice apart from two points of fire just below the curve of his jaw. 'Let me help you,' Gideon whispered, words slurred. 'I'm sorry if it hurts.'

The darkened insides of the Maroubra Bay Hotel smoothed into the flat surface of a calm sea. Joe stared down at his reflection, moonlit this time, pale and looking dead. It screamed at him and thrashed, smacking against water like a tinted windowpane.

'Doesn't hurt—' Joe started to say. Then something clenched inside him. His heart, he thought, beating strangely, smacking against his ribs. But more than that. It was his life, his old self, everything that could have been, everything he had lost, diving back inside him like needles through the two points on his neck. And he gasped, shuddered, tried to pull away. But Gideon held him, and his demon-reflection screamed.

'Not yet.' Gideon's voice cracked. The sea and the pub flickered over each other like a bad photoshop job and Joe strained to look down at the demon, pressed against his neck. Streams of bright tears trailed down Gideon's smooth, pale jaw. 'Not until I free you from your demon. From the darkness that hurts so much.'

Joe, head fuzzy from the sea and stomach rebelling with the beer, leaned into Gideon and wrapped ungainly arms around him. He hugged the demon, as the demon hugged him, patting his back. 'It's okay, mate. Don't worry about it. You don't have to do that. Not for me.'

Gideon drew back and stared at him. Blood and tears mingled on his chin.

'Can see you don't want to, mate,' Joe said. He held the hem of an inner sleeve against his neck until the bleeding stopped. He healed quickly, since the demon took him, but everything left terrible scars. 'So – don't.'

'I—' Gideon sounded confused. Strange, for a demon to be confused. 'I thought you hated the demon. I thought you hated what it did to your life.'

Joe shrugged. 'Well, yeah. Of course I do.'

'And this is the only way I can help you! I told you: you can't replace what you have lost by searching in the sand. Even if you find yourself, you can never reclaim it all, not while that demon sits so contentedly inside you.'

'What?'

'The demon took those parts of you and wedged itself in their place.' Gideon made useless, circular motions with his hands, and they still sounded like wings. 'That's what they do.'

'Oh.' Joe scratched at the scars on his arm, the ones that rose up all over his body like goddamned tectonic plates were having a field day beneath his skin. Were all those evenings dredging through the sand an utter waste of time?

'That demon's in you, now, and while you are alive nothing can dislodge it. While you are alive, you will never be free.'

'While I am alive.' Joe looked up and finally understood. Gideon *was* a demon, after all. 'You were killing me?'

Gideon wrung his fluttering hands at his chest, so hard he shed fresh sheets of dust with the motion. 'Eating you, actually.'

And yet, Joe had seen tears. 'Then why'd you cry like

that?'

'It's lonely in the sea at night,' Gideon said again, voice small and quiet. 'I was going to eat you and free you, like I do for all the others I find. But then you started talking about the sea like that. You offered me chips. You called me mate. And I dared to believe, for a moment, that you were different. That you really were like me, and we could be friends. But one mate shouldn't eat the other, am I right?'

'Yeah.'

'So we can't be mates, then. Because I can't help you if I don't kill you, and mates should always help each other if they can, shouldn't they?' Gideon wrapped himself in shadow like a child clinging to a blanket.

Joe, more than a little intoxicated, contemplated death. Nothingness. No scars, no stench, no memories that haunted him in the daylight and no desperation that fuelled him after dusk. His lonely, demon-torn life hardly compared.

But Gideon was right. Mates shouldn't eat each other, even with the best intentions. And they didn't leave each other depressed and all alone, either.

Maybe this dark scrap of a life might be better, with company.

'No beer when you're dead, I imagine.' Joe scratched at the crawling things in his hair. 'And no one to share it with.'

Gideon shook his head. 'Not the kind of death that I would send you to, at least.'

Joe lifted surprised eyebrows. 'There's more than one?'

'Indeed.' Hope in the demon's eyes. 'There are many.'

'You could tell me about them, if you like. Over another beer.' Joe grinned. Didn't matter if he showed the rotting stubs of what was left of his teeth to a demon with breath like Gideon's. 'Your shout, of course.'

'Of course.' This time, when Gideon smiled, he let his fangs hang out.

Cold Beneath the Bougainvillea

Each night the cat buries herself, cold at the back of my knee. Ice seeps onto my skin through thick blankets. She arranges stiff limbs. Her hard paws are clogged with grit, claws dull as she kneads my thigh. She cleans grey, matted fur with a grave-digging sound.

I hold the duvet tight around my neck. She will stay, if I am still. She will not wander the lonely night.

Morning and she is back beside the shed, ridged body sprinkled red with bougainvillea blooms. Creatures crawl from empty eyes, filth festers beneath her tail.

I do not move her, even as her body rots away.

So she can bury herself. With me.

Simulation Theory

Mike's brains are in his helmet and they make this weird sound – slosh slosh slosh – as Ned runs. The mountains are copper shadows, the ground dark and bloody, and the sky burns. Knopp hollers in his ear, all static and distance and panic. He knows they're shooting above him, behind him, but all he can hear is brains. And Knopp. And Tucka, out there, somewhere, screaming.

He won't let them hurt Tucka too.

Ned runs. Bullets snap at his feet, sing past his ear. Tucka is a shadow in the smoke, the bulb from his camera sharply red, the desperate lights from his hub ports flashing blue. His tracks scream as he fights the sand, stuck in who the fuck knows what and why the fuck did he pick now to malfunction?

The roar of helicopter blades cut through everything. The flash of missile fire. Then the ground's rolling, and there's pain down his back, and Ned falls. He can't move. Mike's helmet rolls away, sloshing. And Ned can't do anything. As the bullets rip through Tucka, shatter camera lens, tear steel sheeting, rip out wires like guts. All he can do is scream—

.   .   .

'Sergeant!'

Ned slammed his head back against the chair rest and his robot arm jerked wildly. The cup he'd worked so hard just to pick up went flying, smashing into the far wall, leaving a solid crack in the plaster. Sweat ran down his face, and the chair beeped furiously as it fought to normalise his heart rate and breathing.

'Edward?' Beth, his nurse, leaned in close. 'What happened?' Those hard brown eyes searched his face, even as she reached around and fiddled with the nodes in the back of his head.

Shivers coursed through him, the world seemed to shake a little, with every movement she made.

'Pointless,' he spat the word, didn't care about the drool dribbling down his chin. What dignity did he have left anyway?

That stopped her. She sat back, lips pinched to white. 'That's enough of that kind of talk.' Bitch didn't have the decency to treat him like the pathetic invalid he was. Beth walked over to the wall, collected the cup and replaced it on the table next to his arm. 'Try again.'

Except it wasn't his arm, now was it? It was a part of the chair. Ugly motorised contraption on wheels, with a high back to strap him into, and nightmarish steel arms a mix of scorpion pincers and black skeleton bones.

'No,' he whispered.

'Now come on. You've been doing so well. Concentrate, and you can control the chair all on your own. Start by imagining—'

'I said no!' Ned shouted. He was sick of her prattle. Imagine moving his arm, imagine lifting the cup, the nodes in his brain and their connection to the chair will do the rest.

What good would imagining do? He couldn't imagine the shrapnel out of his spine. He couldn't imagine everyone in his unit back to life. He couldn't imagine Tucka in one piece. So what was the fucking point of it all?

They should have let him die.

'Try again, Ned.'

Ned's heart would have skipped a beat if the chair wasn't regulating it for him. For a moment, the world shook again, and Knopp's voice was in his ear and Mike's brains were in his hands. Then Beth turned him around to face his Captain, standing casually in the doorway. She looked odd, in civvies. Skirt and shirt and heels, all pressed and clean and polished.

'Sir,' Ned whispered. His robot arm twitched, an involuntary almost-salute that embarrassed him even more.

'This isn't like you, Sergeant.' Captain Knopp crouched beside the chair. She looked tired, grey streaks in her short hair, lines deep in her sun-spotted face. But she was smiling, and she met his gaze, and didn't look with pity or disgust on his useless body. 'You're a damned good soldier, Ned. And you belong in the field. Can't go back out there if you give up, can you?'

'Field?' he asked, voice cracked. 'What could I possibly do in the field now?'

'What you've always done so well.' Knopp stood, and wheeled his chair around while Beth altered the angle of his neck brace so he could see the floor.

There, rolling into the room on newly-clean treads, was Tucka.

'That's—' Ned felt lightheaded, like he wasn't even breathing. 'That's impossible.' He'd watched Tucka die. Just like the rest of his mates, his whole fucking unit, ambushed in the middle of an IED recovery. Tucka's brains might be circuits and his skin steel, but dead was dead, just the same.

'Only as impossible as you are,' Knopp said.

Ned almost didn't hear her. He was so deeply focused on Tucka, taking in every familiar scratch, every patched-up dent, and the dog tags he and Mike had wielded to Tucka's chassis. The bomb disposal robot had saved his life, and the life of everyone in his unit, at least a dozen times. Ned would recognise him anywhere.

'I knew you could do this,' Knopp was saying. 'I knew paralysis and brain damage wouldn't stop you.'

One of Ned's robotic arms was lifting, almost on its own, to reach for Tucka. Like he could touch him, pat him, and make sure he was real. 'Tucka, mate.' He swore the robot's camera was looking right back. He could feel it.

'You're moving a machine with your mind, Ned. Have you thought about how fucking amazing that is? Because you should. And that's just the beginning of what your new and improved brain is capable of.'

Ned frowned at his extended arm. He pinched the clawed hand into a rough fist. 'Improved?'

'Your nodes, Edward,' Beth said, behind him. 'They patch up a hole in the back of your skull, the link between your chair and the electrical impulses from your brain. But they can do so much more.'

'And it's time to put that to the test,' Knopp said. 'I need you back in the field, Sergeant. That's an order.'

He tried to swallow, but his useless throat got stuck halfway.

'But you won't be on your own.'

He was still stuck in the bloody chair.

Beth was off to the side somewhere, doing something he couldn't see. 'Establishing connection to your cortex array, Edward,' she was saying, talking to him when he couldn't look her in the eye. 'Just relax. This will feel a little strange at first.'

'Where's Tucka?' he asked, again. He'd lost count of the

number of times he'd asked her, since she hoisted him out of his bed and strapped him into his chair. Lost count of the number of times she refused to answer.

'Just focus, Edward. The transition will be a shock. Remember to keep calm.'

'But I need to know—'

And suddenly the room was gone. Beth too. Even the fucking chair. And Ned, breathless, stunned, looked up to mountains he knew so well. Those same copper shadows, stretching into the glass sky, looming over him. He couldn't breathe. Logar Province. How did he get back here? He didn't understand, what the fuck was going on?

Beth's words were ringing through his head, almost like he could still hear her urging him to keep calm. He tried to take a deep breath, but he didn't have lungs. He looked down, to his stupid useless body, and found Tucka's battered steel casing instead.

He wasn't alone.

He was keenly aware of every inch of the robot, more aware than he'd ever been, even after so many years of working so closely together. Ned had never been a soldier's soldier. Not good at all that team bonding, running for ages with heavy packs on your back bullshit. What Ned was good at was machines. And Tucka was his favourite. Standard run of the mill bomb disposal unit when he was first allocated, but under Ned's guidance, Tucka had become something else. Overclocked, extra sensors, heightened interactivity. One of the team. More than that. One of the boys.

But now, Ned could *feel* the grit in Tucka's treads and the hunger of his reduced battery life. He could see through his camera, comprehend the data in his satellite feeds and he knew, a feeling deep inside his bones, that Tucka was waiting for Ned to tell him what to do.

'Tucka, mate,' he whispered. Or didn't. He couldn't tell.

Together, their camera focused on a bulky object in the middle of the dodgy dirt road. A car, wired up to blow them all to hell. In place of the fear of his waking nightmares, Ned felt a deep satisfaction. A sense that this was right.

'Just like old times.'

Under Ned's direction, Tucka rolled forward. They approached the IED with caution. Dimly, Ned could hear gunfire and voices, but they weren't his problem. Him and Tucka, they were here for the bomb. They quickly located a simple proximity fuze, and cast a smothering net to disable its twin seismic and magnetic sensors. This was Tucka's specialty. A quick dump of data that confused the bomb's tiny processors, paralysing it for just long enough, while he dug through the confused mess of decoy wiring, found the detonator and removed the striker-pin—

And everything went blank.

Ned woke to an impossible sensation of wetness. His hands were dripping. Holding Mike's sloshing helmet, and dripping—

'Edward?' Beth appeared in front of his face. This time, there wasn't any hardness in her eyes, the cold stone glare that refused his protests and forced him to practice with his robot arms. She was smiling. 'Back with us, I see?'

He opened his mouth, but before he could say a word she placed a straw inside it, and he realised he was so damned thirsty. His throat was raw and dry, like he had swallowed half a desert's worth of sand.

'Good boy,' she said, and stroked the side of his cheek as he sucked down great mouthfuls of water. 'You did so well.' She placed a soft kiss just beneath his eye, and took the straw away.

He frowned at her, but she disappeared down, out of his

vision. 'What are you doing?' Silence beat around him. 'Where am I?' He thought he was in the chair but it was hard to tell. Something was supporting his neck, and he'd been angled back, looking up. He didn't recognise the lime-green ceiling.

'Shhh,' Beth whispered. He tried to move his head, to look down, but he was strapped tightly. 'Relax, you've earned it. I'm here to look after you.'

'Earned it?' Uncertainty danced in his belly. She sounded right next to him. Was she touching him? He couldn't tell, couldn't feel a thing, except for the phantom wetness across his hands. 'How did I earn it? Beth? Please, look at me?'

A little sigh, and she was back. Close to his face. 'You must remember,' she said. 'Out in the field. You did such a good job.'

He did? What field? 'But where am I now? How long have I been here?'

Instead of answering, Beth gave him another drink. Her fingertips smelled like blood, and oil.

Tucka edged forward, cautiously. Quiet and empty-looking now, but Ned couldn't help but remember the last time they'd been in this village. An insurgent hideout. Blood on the white-plastered walls. The goat Mike accidentally shot, wailing as it died slowly. Kids clustered at the front door, terrified faces and huge eyes, but bastards with guns hiding in the shadows behind them.

What do you do? How do you know? Knopp'd wanted to send in Tucka, to check. Afterwards, Ned hadn't slept for a week.

Now, the place was ghostly. No kids in the broken door, pile of bones where the goat might have been, bullet holes in all the walls. And they were sending Tucka back in. At least this time, Ned could go with him.

'That's it, mate. Nice and slow.'

What were they looking for, again? It was hard to keep track of the specifics, but Tucka seemed to know what he was doing. His flexible, all-terrain tracks carried them up a short set of stairs, and rolled silently across cement floor. Cold air brushed over them, Ned could feel it crisp against Tucka's metallic skin. It felt like air-conditioning, but that couldn't be right, could it? Not here.

Around a corner – he didn't remember the hallways being so wide – and there it was, the 9M96E component of the *S-400 Triumf*, an old-school soviet surface to air intercept missile, just lying there live and dangerous. Yes. That's what they were after. Even as Tucka hurried over and began deactivating it, almost of his own volition, Ned began to wonder. Who would leave this here, in an empty room? With smooth floors, and clean walls—

—*'E.A.T.R.'S got interference on the signal. Run me a quick diagnostic'*—

For a moment Tucka and the compound and the missile were gone. Ned was in his chair and Beth was there, talking to a bunch of wankers in labcoats, worry in her eyes this time, her gestures wild and sweeping.

Then he was back with Tucka, and the missile, a section of its warhead hanging open, and the anti-handling device already disengaged. Yes, that was better. That was what they were here to do. Diffuse and collect. So he reached down with Tucka's great mechanical arms, just like collecting a cup with the ones attached to his chair.

But Tucka wouldn't budge.

—*'I know it's almost done, but I still think we should abort! I'm not liking the look of these numbers.'*— Beth's voice.

The robot backed away, spun suddenly on its tracks and headed for the open doorway.

'Tucka, mate?' Ned whispered. His lips were so dry they'd split in the corner, and there was cold air blowing on Tucka's camera. Both, at once. 'What are you doing?' Fear rattled through him. Dimly, he could hear voices, but the words were hazy, coming in and out of focus. Beth. Knopp. Others he didn't know. All freaking the fuck out. 'Please. Stop.'

Tucka told him not to be such a pussy. So clearly Ned could almost hear the words. And Ned couldn't help but laugh, a short snort that wiped all his fear away, instantly. 'Fuck you, Tucka,' he chuckled.

Somewhere, a warning siren blared as his robot carried him deep into the ruined compound, deeper than they'd ever been before. The further they went, the less like Ned's memory it became. Cement floor was replaced by pale ceramic tiles, strips of fluorescent lights embedded high in walls, numbers painted above gun metal grey doors. What was this place? At the same time, Beth was leaning in close, eye to eye, calling his name.

— *'Ned. Ned. Can you hear me?'* —

Tucka came to a halt inside a small dark room, with a gaping crater at its centre. He skirted around the shattered tiles and broken cement to something on the far side. A hole blasted in the wall. He flicked on his low level light imaging, and peered inside.

'Tucka's treasure,' Ned breathed the words.

—*'But you said there were protocols to follow to avoid permanent damage to his mind!'*—

There was the piece of shrapnel Mike had wielded into a makeshift helmet to fit over Tucka's camera. The bottle of beer they'd given the robot for New Years – still full. Bits and pieces he'd collected himself over the years. Rocks and twig, chunks of rubble. An old mirror. Anything that had, apparently, taken the robot's fancy and he'd kept, rather than consuming as fuel for his engines. The snow hadn't survived the trip home.

Ned knew this because Tucka was telling him. In flashes of memory and electrical spikes that surged through him like emotion. Tucka reached in with a careful pincer and withdrew his most precious treasure.

—*'Fine, do it then, but hurry up'*—

Ned had once made Tucka a medal, after he'd seen them safely through the Tera Pass. Out of a flattened bottle cap and a scrap of silver insulation, Tucka's name and the date scratched on the surface. Half-joking, half-absolutely serious. And here it was, kept safe.

'And you call *me* a pussy?' Ned whispered, but he was smiling. It felt like the robot was smiling too.

The alarms were getting worse. 'Come on, mate,' Ned said. 'We have to get back.' Tucka gave him control again. Together, they retraced the machine's tracks. 'It's okay,' Ned hoped he was saying out loud, but he had no way of really knowing. 'We're coming back. You can all calm down.'

—*'Just try not to do any damage'*—

But this time, one of the steel doors was open.

'Wait!' Ned jerked his head – their head – to one side, and Tucka's grip on his vision – their vision – wavered.

Dimly, Ned could see Beth's close-up face replaced by Knopp, eyes red-rimmed and nervous.

Then he was back with Tucka. In Tucka. The robot slowed, swivelled his camera, allowing Ned to get a better look through the open door. Bodies, strung up in chairs, bound to machines, but not the way he was. Robotic arms clamped to inflamed shoulders, robotic legs drilled into exposed hipbones. Tucka zoomed in on a single face.

'Mike? Is that you?' He was certain, even with only one

eye remaining and most of his mouth turned to metal. He'd have known his mate anywhere.

—*'Disconnecting in five, four'*—

'No, wait please!' Ned urged Tucka forward. Men walked through the rows of bodies, all dressed in black and carrying guns. Who were they? Their faces were covered, insignia obscured.

—*'Three, two'*—

Tucka's camera wavered. The image began to turn to snow. Together, Ned and Tucka reached for Mike. Mike who's brains Ned had carried. Mike who stared down at them both, shock on his face so terribly alive.

—*'One.'*—

Beth washed the sweat from his body with a sponge and bucket. 'The technical term, Edward, is PTSD.'

Ned opened his eyes and looked down at where she was scrubbing his feet. She'd draped a towel over his crotch. It's maintenance, he thought, watching her fingers move so steady and precise.

'What—?' he tried to ask, but his mouth was dry again. His lips hurt.

Beth sighed, gave up cleaning and crouched beside his head. She ran soft fingers just below his hairline. Touched him where he could feel it.

'It's nothing to be ashamed of.' As she spoke, her fingers traced along his face. They dipped down to his neck, then disappeared.

What was she doing?

He swallowed and coughed and forced himself to speak. His raw throat tasted of blood. 'How did I get here?' He recognised the bed, and the pulley that got him out and into the chair every morning. But he had no memory of coming here.

'Memory loss is common.' She kissed his cheek. 'Just relax.' She kissed his mouth. 'I'm here to look after you.' She was very warm.

'But I saw—'

'Nightmares.' Where were her hands? He had the sudden impression the cloth around his groin was gone, even though he couldn't feel it. 'I will help you forget them.' Her mouth was on his chin now, his neck, going down—

'No,' he whispered through cracked lips.

He closed his eyes. And he couldn't feel what else she might have done. He didn't want to know.

In the darkness behind his eyelids he could still see the images from Tucka's camera feed. Mike's half a face, and all the other bodies, behind his.

They were back on a dodgy dirt road. The mountains seemed closer, larger, looming and too brightly red. In front of them, another wrecked car wired into an IED. Sounds of fighting coming from… somewhere. Behind them? Off to the side? Guns hidden in the haze, the smoke from bombs obscuring any details of friend or foe.

Tucka rolled forward, confident, ready. This was what they were made for, the two of them, together.

'Wait,' Ned whispered, and wondered just who could hear him. Tucka slowed, turned his camera, scanned the road, the desert, the mountains. 'How did we get here?' Where was the rest of the convoy? The transport trucks, the armoured jeeps. 'When—?'

For an instant, the mountains shuddered, replaced by the bullet-riddled compound walls. Static and snow gnawed at their edges. He blinked. Mountains again. Closer than before.

Ned goaded Tucka to focus in on the blackened, twisted remains of a tree silhouetted against the hard blue sky, that simply hadn't been there before.

'What—?'

Beth's face, again. Close, again. —*'Dammit'*—

Tucka ignored the tree, and rolled on. They had a job to do. The most important job of all. Find the bombs, stop the bombs. Keep everyone safe. And then they will love you. And they will praise you. As long as you keep them safe.

'Everyone?' Ned whispered, to himself, to Tucka, to Beth? What did it matter? 'Who is there to keep safe?' His mates were dead, or were they half-alive, hooked up like monsters to terrible machines. Which one was he?

Tucka didn't care. As long as he had Ned, as long as they were working. Tucka didn't care. And neither should Ned.

—*'We only abort if there's no other option'*—

As Tucka closed in on the bomb, Ned steadied himself. The robot took the lead, began suppressing, scanning. Tracing the patterns of wire and explosive and circuitry to find the detonator.

—*'There, see, that's better'*—

Ned listened to the distant gunfire. He felt the heat of the sun. The grit between Tucka's treads seemed so real. But as the robot reached in, pincers ready, Ned wrestled back control. He retracted their suppression field and dragged the camera away from the bomb, forced it to aim at the impossible tree.

Tucka fought back. What was he doing? Didn't he want to help everyone?

'It's too late for that,' Ned gasped, and pushed Tucka forward.

The proximity fuze sensed them with a squeal and a surge of data, and the world flashed white.

.   .   .

The mountains were copper, the ground dark and bloody, the sky thick with smoke. And all of it flickered on loop across two battered old tv screens. Ned blinked, frowned at them. Scratching gunfire, distant explosions, the whirr of a helicopter low overhead. His gaze slid down to small array of speakers beneath the screens.

'What—?' he tried to speak. But there was something in his mouth.

'Well that answers that,' Beth said, and walked across his line of sight, tapping at the tablet she was carrying. Didn't even look at him.

'It was worth a try.' That was Knopp's voice, but he couldn't see her. She sounded resigned. Defeated.

'Even if the outcome was predicable.' Beth placed her tablet down beside the screens and turned them off, one by one. The desert mountains replaced by darkness. The gunfire by a deeper, machine hum. Then she approached Ned. Her hard eyes didn't meet his gaze, not even briefly. They scanned his chair, they looked over the top of his head as she reached over to mess with his nodes. 'But of course you're right, Sir.'

He couldn't speak. Couldn't even swallow. There was something in his mouth, and down his throat. Hard and uncomfortable. He wished he could gag. His lips felt stretched, dry. Cracked.

'Do what you have to do,' Knopp said, followed by the sound of heels, clicking down tiled floors.

Sweat down his face. Panicking, he glanced around, to the dead screens, the unfamiliar ceiling, and Beth. He pleaded with her, silently, to meet his gaze, to do something to help him.

But she didn't even look his way, and her face remained impassive. 'Get him prepped for the next stage,' she said.

And then he was moving. Gliding. Still in his chair? Away

from the screens, past banks of computers and clusters of men and women in white labcoats. One, all dressed in black, gun in hand.

He almost didn't notice Tucka.

A pile of broken machinery wedged in the corner. His camera shattered, his tracks all loose, mechanical body riddled with bullet holes, but his dog tags still intact. They glinted, his name crisp beneath fluorescent lights. Countless snake-piles of wires ran out of him, into the computers, and pipes of coolant connected him to the wall, and every so often, one of his delicate pincers twitched.

'Tucka!' Ned choked around the thing in his mouth. 'Tucka!' But he could barely make a sound. So he reached with the chair's mechanical arms, the ones Beth had worked so hard to teach him how to use. And he reached for his robot, the deep connection between them.

But nothing happened.

He was wheeled away, out of the room, away from Tucka.

And he could do nothing.

He undoes the buttons, slowly, one by one. Then peels us off. Hands that were so hurtful only a moment before are soft, are gentle. They smooth us, they rub us, they caress. We know the feeling. From smaller, manicured fingers we have felt it before. Beneath store lights, hanging from cold wire.

A shudder runs through us as he shakes us, spreads us open. He studies us, down to our very last thread. Eyes red-rimmed, darting; cheeks fevered beneath stubble. Then a small cry from lips far too wet.

He turns to look at her sprawled on the floor. We can see her too. There is blood from her hands and it has come off on us. Just a little around the left sleeve.

Cursing, he kicks her bare leg. His hands around her neck had not left a scratch, no blood to mar us. But she fought him too hard to allow that. Her fingernails tore and her knuckles bled, and she left her final mark.

It is a small victory, one that can be undone with suds and scrubbing. So he goes to it. The sink is cold; it is polished silver and freshly bought soap. The water chills us. The room is too white, the sink too clean. The body on the floor too dead. Her hair is a splash of black against pale tiles.

Finally, he turns the tap and pats the sleeve dry. As he smooths our newly-made wrinkles, with hands inexpert compared to her loving touch, we whisper.

Just among ourselves. Just for now.

He leaves her body naked on the floor, steps over her without another glance. There is a door behind the white hanging towels, and beyond it…beyond it is our new home.

A long room, just as clean as the bathroom. No, cleaner. Benches of steel without a smudge, and on them large cases made of glass, each the height of a woman, give or take a head or leg. Within them our siblings.

Still carrying us, still staring at us, he passes them all. A child of wispy white, of gauze and feathers. A harlot in leather and ruby. And even an old lady, dark with lace and age. Well cared for, well loved, now pinned beneath fluorescents. We hear them all, whispering, hissing to each other. They fog spotless glass with fury and warn us.

That is when we understand. We are all he was ever after. She fought, died and will be discarded because of us. Who looked after us so well.

Surrounded by voices, beaten by lights and fearing the glass, we whisper. With all the voices we can muster, we whisper. We reach with threads, with lint, toward his fingers, hoping he will hear us.

Do not let us go.

He stops at the bench, at an open and empty case. Gently, he lowers us to metal, smooths us, arranges. Fixing a notch in the collar, a twist in the belt. One of the tiny bows near the neck has slipped, so he tightens it just enough. Compares it to its partner.

Does he feel it squeeze his finger? He slips away, cobalt

satin is not strong enough to hold him. But he stares at us still. Does not lock us away. And all the while we whisper.

Won't you let us hold you?

Fingers trace embroidery that looked so pretty against her chest; vibrant flowers, a tiny bird in pink and white. They follow our buttons down, past the thin belt, right to the hem. There he flips us open, a small gesture, like a playful lover.

Won't you wear us?

His hands move but his eyes are riveted on us. On the bird. His shirt soon falls to the floor. His chest is smooth and well shaped; as neat as his bathroom, as organised as his collection. Then his pants and shoes are gone. We know how much he desires us. How much he wants us to hold him.

The others have stopped whispering. They are holding their breath beneath coffins of glass.

We want to hold you.

He slips us over his shoulders. His skin is soft and smells of soap and oils. He is broad, far bigger than she, but we can stretch for this. We can lose our shape, we can ruin our beauty. Anything, for this.

We fit around his arms, wrap around his chest and waist. He does each button back up, breath deep and husky. Soon he is fumbling, desperate to close us. The belt fights him, turns from his fingers and he does not bother to tie it.

We will hold you.

As he gasps and groans we tighten. His heat fills us, his pleasure sullies us, but still we tighten. And, for a moment, he smiles.

We will hold you tightly.

Still we squeeze. A button pops, flying to the far corner of the room, its clattering against the floor a death-cry. But we have come too far to stop. The belt closes. It squeezes high, as close to his chest as it can reach. Pushes air from his lungs in a sharp gust.

And we will never let you go.

He knows something is wrong now. He tugs at us, pulls at us with fingers made desperate again. This time by fear. Sleeves squeeze the blood from his arms; his hands drop useless and blue. He screams. Falls to the floor and kicks blood onto the tiles.

We will keep you.

The bows untie, and reach for his red, straining face.

Just like this.

Satin slivers easily along his neck, over jaw and cheekbones.

Forever.

To find his eyes.

As we squeeze.

Mirror Dirt

I wipe the bathroom mirror with a Windex-soaked cloth but the dirt always comes back. Not the next day, not the next week, but right after the cloth passes by.

Jody stands behind me, holding a dark towel. It droops to the tiled floor like a shroud.

'Just cover the damned thing, Helen.' She makes a face and it comes out distorted in the mirror dirt. Skin the grey pallor of old chalk, tongue loose over her chin. The mirror has taken her eyes again, too. It has a thing for eyes.

'There's got to be a way to clean this thing!' I rub until the joint in my elbow aches. In the end we resort to the towel.

It doesn't take long for the mirror dirt to spread to other rooms.

'Mountains, definitely.' Jody crosses her arms as she stares at the mirror on my wardrobe door. The growing landscape freaks me out so much I can't get to my clothes.

'What about yours?'

She shrugs, eyes slide away from mine. 'Just dirt. Like the one in the bathroom. You're lucky, you got pretty scenery.'

I suppose she's right. But when Jody leaves, something moves. Reaching in to find a shirt, I'm close enough to see the detail. Horses on a mountain trail, with people riding them.

Jody covers all the mirrors in her bedroom. A sheet for the wardrobe, another towel for the one on her dresser. I've grown accustomed to mine; trees that rock in the breeze, the continual trail of horses and people along the mountains.

'How can you sleep with *that*?' Jody won't step inside my room anymore. Not since clouds materialized above the mountain range and rained condensation onto the carpet.

'It's peaceful.'

Jody is pale, the long-life bulb in the hallway sucking life and color from her face. 'It isn't right.'

I haven't tried to clean my mirror; they're just mountains after all.

'You should cover it.' Her sentence ends in a yawn.

Green blossoms on the mountain slopes as she trudges out to work. I've already called in sick.

I wake to darkness and knocking. The tinny rap of a hand against glass.

When I turn on the light the mountains are heavy with mist. I peel off damp sheets and step onto squelching carpet. As I walk past the mirror I see a figure, hazy and still, on the trail. Too tiny to tell, really, but I feel like it's watching me.

I head to the bathroom to wash sweat off my face. In the silence, after the tap has dripped its last, I hear sobbing. Not tinny, not hidden behind glass, but muffled behind wood. Jody?

I take a half step toward her room. But she is silent, if I ever heard her.

Back to the bathroom mirror, I pull off her towel to dry my face. This mirror dirt has become a graveyard. I cover it again, hurriedly, when the earth starts to move.

There are too many empty graves.

The figure is still there in the morning. A little closer, perhaps. I peer at it, with my nose against the mirror, but cannot make it out.

I'm in the kitchen before I realise Jody is still in bed.

I knock on her door, the sound comes away hollow.

'Jody?' I turn the knob and gradually push my way in.

Clothes litter the floor in her room, her sheets are torn and pillows gutted. Her bedside lamp with its silly pink frill is broken on the floor.

Why didn't I hear it drop?

I find Jody lying beside her bed. Just as I reach her, as I crouch to turn her over, something whispers behind my ear.

'Too late.'

That's when I realize the mirrors are uncovered.

I look up to faces leering out of the glass. They grin at me, great vacant eyes and mouths without teeth. Like they belong in the bathroom cemetery.

'You're too late.' The voice comes from the mirror on her chest of drawers. 'Go back to your mountains, Helen.' Jody's voice. 'Go back and wait.'

I turn her body over, my hands shaking. 'No.' The tears finally come as I look into her blank face. Like a mirror, it's smooth and empty. I can see only myself.

'You got the nice one.' Her body is cold.

From my room, I hear knocking. A hand against glass.

Little Ghost Boy

The little ghost boy sits on the edge of the cliff, playing a borrowed DS. His semi-transparent feet dangle over the sea. He likes *Nintendogs* the best, doesn't care if it's supposed to be a girl's game. He always wanted a dog of his own.

Cassie meets the boy by accident; she is actually hiding from Robert. She has had enough of the way he pinches her arms, steps on her shoes, and pulls her blonde pigtail.

'You should be careful.' The little ghost boy does not look up. His puppy is good at catching frisbees; they have been practicing all night. 'You could fall.'

'I won't.' Cassie sits beside him. She has never seen a dead boy so closely. Cold wind from the sea flutters her maroon skirt. She holds it between her knees. 'Shouldn't you be out there?' she asks, and points to the dead riding the waves below them.

'No.' Some of the dead are surfing. More of them bob further out on improvised flotsam rafts, or simply tread water. 'Don't like to swim. It's wet.' His DS won't work under water.

'But the dead belong in the ocean.' Everyone knows that.

Even as they speak, shadows form in the shoals. Silent, large and threatening. When the cry goes up, when the surfers drag their limbs onto boards and the swimmers kick frantically for the rafts it is too late.

The little ghost boy turns his face away. 'And it's scary.'

The death that rears large-mouthed and alien from the sea is a final death. Indiscriminate, emotionless, it swallows mouthfuls of the deceased before easing softly back into the ocean.

They will not return.

The waters clear. The rafts bob. Surfers hunt for the swell.

Cassie does not understand why the little ghost boy should fear death. He is already dead. But she does not tell him that, because she has already worked out that he could be useful.

'You will have to go in one day,' she says.

'Won't.' But the little ghost boy's hand shakes. He grips the plastic stylus hard.

'You will. All the dead do.' She watches him play his game. 'Janey's dog had puppies a few weeks ago.' She dangles the words like bait on a line. 'They're really cute. She let me go and pat them.'

He sits so still. His dog begs.

'A real dog is better than a pretend one.' She stands, runs hands over the sand clinging to the back of her school uniform. 'Like a real boy is better than a dead one.' And leaves him there.

When Cassie returns his DS is folded shut on the stone beside his legs.

He waits for her to sit down, but she remains behind him. He watches the swimmers, remembers the sucking of water and the weight of it over his head. He will never go back in there. Not even now, when he has no air left for the water to take. He might be dead, but it is still dangerous.

'Can I see the puppies?' He does not look at Cassie. She stands behind him, red and white polka-dot dress bright in the sun. He does not like her. He was happy, with his DS, if she had only left him alone. Like everyone else does. The joggers on the beach path, the couples looking for scrub to hide them; one look at the little dead boy and they hurry away. No one likes to get too close to a ghost.

'Only if you do something for me,' she answers. He is not surprised.

'I told you I'm not going in there.'

'I don't want you to.' She holds out her hand. 'Come with me, and I will show you what I want you to do.'

The little boy stands. He tucks his DS into his shorts. He looks at her palm, so solid and pink where his is transparent and slightly blue. 'You are brave. Everyone else is afraid of me.'

And she smiles, a look that makes him like her even less. Her teeth are little, white and perfect. 'I know you won't touch me. So I have nothing to fear.'

They squeeze through the fence together; it is easier for him than Cassie. She catches her hem on a salt-rusted crack in the tubing, and tears her dress. She doesn't seem to care. The little boy thinks this is strange.

'Are you taking me to the puppies?'

They follow the side of the road. Cassie crosses it like a grown up would, easy and without fear. He hurries to keep up with her and wishes he could hold her hand, just for the roads.

'How long have you been sitting there?' She does not answer his question.

He shakes his head. 'I don't remember.' He touches the DS in his pocket and wishes his dog was by his side.

'What was your name?'

'I don't remember.'

Cassie walks with determination, up a hill, through back streets and lanes. 'Being dead is pretty horrible then, isn't it? You aren't who you were, you can't be who you might have been. All you can do is swim.' She smiles at him, does not know he hates to see her do it. 'Or watch the others swim, at least.'

'It is.' But he is not sure about that. He remembers his mother holding his hand as they crossed the street, going to the pool that day. He remembers dogs playing, and wishing one of them was his. But not much else. So really, he has little to compare it to.

'Good.'

Cassie leads him to a park. It is small, boxed by wooden fences, and no one but Robert, with his older brother and his friends, comes here.

Cassie enjoys the thrill of knowing she should not be here, just as she did the first time. When she followed Robert to see what he would do. He pulled the elastics out of her hair, ripped her dress, and scraped her knees on cement. Then he took her shoes, tied the laces together and hung them from the electricity wires. They dangle still.

His petty cruelties disappointed her. But walking home in dirty socks, holding her favourite dress together, she had decided he was bad enough.

To bring the little ghost boy here.

'Do you see the shorter one? The fat one? With ugly red hair?' She rolls the insults around like a lolly, forbidden and sweet.

'Yes.' The little ghost boy answers quietly.

'I want you to touch him.'

A breeze flaps Cassie's dress, but not the dead boy's shorts.

'No.'

'If you don't, I won't show you Janey's puppies.'

'No.'

'Just touch him. He can't hurt you.'

'But I can hurt him.' And that's why the joggers, the couples, all hurry quickly away. Maybe that is why the rest of the ghosts swim, separate from the alive world.

Death is contagious.

It's also why he can't understand that Cassie does not fear him. Why she would even hold her hand out to him, tempting death and smiling.

'Do it!'

The boys have seen them. But they do not laugh and surround Cassie with the little ghost boy beside her. They are quiet, still in ways their parents would never believe possible.

'No!' The little ghost boy runs for the cliff, back the way he has come.

Cassie follows, laughing like a spirit, mad and piercing, echoing from the close walls.

The little ghost boy does not return for three days. Cassie wonders if she has broken him, if he found the courage to join the rest of the dead in the sea. It would be a pity. Although Robert grows quiet every time he sees her now. And he does not pull her hair, and he does not call her horrible names. Maybe the ghost at her side was enough to shut him up.

But it is not enough for Cassie.

So she is glad, when she sees the little ghost boy perched on his spot on the headland above the sea. He does not swing his feet. But he has his DS open.

The little ghost boy could not do it. He tried. He stood on the sand, the water clutching at his feet, and the swimmers gestured to him, opened their arms to him, called him to join them. But his puppy cried, where he balanced it open and shining in the palm of his hand, and he could not do it. The dog relies on him.

So he returned to the cliff, and fed the puppy.

The next day, Cassie brings him a real one.

It dangles from her arms, small and limp, eyes wide open and watching everything. It cries softly, a little whimper, but wags its tail when the boy stands. Maybe it knows a good owner when it sees one; maybe it knows who will love it.

'It's just like you,' Cassie says. 'It doesn't have a name.'

She crouches, helps the dog stand on stubby and wobbly legs. She pats it, deliberately, long, firm strokes. It wiggles in pleasure. It licks, it wags.

The little ghost boy's hands twitch. He longs to touch it, but never will.

'I can bring him back again.' Cassie gives him only a moment to drink the dog in, to bask in its small, warm presence, before scooping it back up. 'But you should do like I asked you. That's only fair.'

And she takes the dog away.

Two days later, she returns. He has worried the whole time.

But she does not pat the puppy. She does not even let him look at it. 'You haven't done your part,' she says, flashing with anger even worse than her smile. 'That's not fair, is it? I brought you the puppy, you should have touched Robert.'

Without another word she takes the puppy back through the fence, down the stairs to the rocks and the sea below.

The little ghost boy watches her, breathless if he had breath, and petrified. As she kneels, as she holds the puppy over the frothing sea, Cassie looks up. 'Well?' she calls, and the little ghost boy, bent and clutching the side of the cliff flinches. 'Hurry! I won't give you long.'

The puppy squirms.

The little ghost boy has no choice. He cannot let the puppy feel what he felt, the sucking cold of water, the horrible fire inside. He is a dog owner. So he runs the way Cassie showed him, across streets and down lanes and between buildings to the park.

And the boys are there – did she know that already?

The little ghost boy does not think about it, he can't. He just runs to them, and in the middle of their laughter turned to sudden screaming he finds the boy Cassie pointed to, the short one, the ugly one, and he wraps a small hand around a much-thicker wrist.

He does not stay to see what happens. He does not gloat over skin washed clean of colour, over eyes turning to blank, over flesh frosting and breath dying. Not the way Cassie would have done.

As he rushes back, and Cassie holds the puppy over the water, she closes her eyes and tries to imagine it. Robert, a ghost in that sea, swallowed up by shadows from below.

When the little ghost boy appears beside her, risking the sea himself for the love of the squirming life in her hands, Cassie smiles her terrifying smile.

'I did it.' He pants, though he does not breathe. He might have forgotten his name, but some things are eternal.

'Then I will give you your reward.' And Cassie dunks the puppy in the sea. She holds it there, while the ghost boy screams and it wriggles, wriggles, and is still.

The little ghost boy sits on the edge of the cliff, patting his little ghost puppy. He laughs as it squirms in his lap, and allows it to lick his face. His DS lies forgotten by his knee, the battery has died.

Neither of them will swim.

Cassie stands on the rocks below. She watches the little ghost boy and his dog, and wonders if he would like another pet, should she ever need him again.

<u>High Density</u>

The deceased estate three doors up was gone by morning, its brick veneer and red tile roof overrun by apartments and secure off-street parking. The young couple who'd just moved in were first home buyers, and hadn't yet built up the memories to protect themselves. We'd watched them arrive, set up regular patrols in the area, even used gifts of home-baked scones and casserole to infiltrate the house.

We fought hard to save them, and would have, if not for me. Carelessness can be deadly on the front line.

Robert carried me home hours before the dawn. 'I'm sorry,' I whispered, head against his shoulder. He was far stronger than a man of almost seventy should have to be, toughened up by war.

He hushed me, the same voice he'd used with Jason all those decades ago, when our son was small and plagued by nightmares. I held tight to that memory. Robert laid me on the couch and ripped open the slacks suddenly tight around my right leg.

'Oh, Alice,' he breathed. 'Love.' Then he ran to the laundry.

I propped myself up on my elbows and stared down at a small balcony growing just below my kneecap, beige paint cracking around my ankle and dimmer switches protruding in a line along my shin.

Robert returned, and shoved a rolled-up drawing Sue had done when she was five into a fresh bottle of bleach. I caught the edges of blue crayon. So powerful a memory, gone, to protect me from my own foolishness.

I'd taken half a bottle of dishwashing liquid and a few earrings to the house three doors up. It simply wasn't enough. Robert had been so confident. 'That Density's only just taking hold,' he'd said. 'We'll be done in a few hours, I'm sure.' And had asked me to make Vegemite sandwiches, in case any of the troops got hungry.

Not his fault. I'd been doing this long enough to know how to prepare myself.

'Keep still,' he said. Then, with memory-infused cleaning agent and a fresh cloth, he rubbed as much of the Density from my leg as he could. But I knew, even as I leaned back and ignored the burning, the scraping, that it would never leave me. Not fully. Once the Density took hold, it was tenacious.

The rest of the patrol returned just after first light. Weapons empty, shoulders sagging, defeat written in exhaustion on their faces. Sometimes, I wondered if we were too old for this fight. But age was the only reason we fought at all.

'Lost it,' Cheryl said. An unlit ciggie jiggled in the corner of her mouth, even at this hour.

'We were too weak,' her husband, Paul, added. At least he didn't look at me.

'Or the Density was too strong,' said Dave, whose wife had died long before the Density began creeping into the street.

Our neighbours and comrades in arms. They didn't stay long.

Robert helped me stand to peer out through the curtains. We watched the final touches go on, three doors up – the honeycomb of dark-glazed windows, hatched with security bars – and a procession of large 4WDs leave the newly installed garage. The young couple drove one of them. Only four days ago they'd arrived in a white, second-hand Corolla.

Robert left for work once most of the traffic was gone, our old station wagon seeming to pass right through the new cars, the clean and slickly black cars, like they were ghosts. Or he was. I was starting to think that we were the shadows now, the unwanted interlopers, even though we had lived here for half a century, bought up when the park across the road was a factory and land was cheap.

The Density was winning. Though we held on with arthritic hands and a lifetime of memories.

It snuck in right after he left. Townhouses, by the look of it. So I took up my broom, wrapped one of the kids' old shirts around the bristles, and swept away faux-terracotta tiles from the hallway floor. With the handle I broke up the beginnings of a birdbath that had sprouted in the lounge room, and dug up stairs leading to an underground carpark growing like mould in the bottom of the bathtub.

My dense leg hurt. Windows were forming above the balcony, stretching up my thigh in sheer glass planes.

During my lonely days at home, I kept the shutters closed and the curtains drawn, because outside of my musty, bleach-smelling house, the world seemed to hum to the Density's urgent tune. Young, plastic-looking mothers jogged behind enormous prams; kids with wheels on their shoes whizzed up and down the street in hunting packs, and cars – so many cars, all so large, all so shiny – roared by. The Density's new world, hurried and blurred.

Robert returned as darkness fell, and only then did we notice that the park on the other side of the road was falling. Concrete bike paths coiled into snake-like cables and folded beneath the earth, benches stretched to scaffolding, and trees inverted into deep foundations. As we rubbed halogen headlights and the beginnings of dark, metallic paint from the front of the station wagon, Robert said, 'Escalation in hostilities. It's surrounding us. Pincer movement. Classic military strategy.'

'That will be a large complex,' I said. Distant jackhammering, like a stubborn insect wail, ate into my words. 'With a pool and a fitness centre.'

'It will?' Robert asked, and for the first time I heard an old-man waver in his voice, and knew he was afraid.

'I can feel it,' I said, and touched my knee.

He paused, shuddered ever so faintly. 'We need to hold a BBQ.'

The next day I bought enough snags to feed an army. It was risky, stepping out to the shops, but I did it early and had time to clear a solar-powered water feature from the gutters. When Saturday came 'round it was obvious I'd bought too many. Our army was dwindling.

Cheryl and Paul came by, of course. They were early, and had smeared jungle paint on their cheeks. They brought the onions and tomato sauce. Then Dave, with a store-bought carrot cake in a plastic container. There were others too, pockets of resistance from the entire length of the street. Pat, a middle-aged spinster – she was the youngest amongst us, but neither looked nor acted it. Lovely old Bill, without the young man who lived with him, and may or may not have been his son. And a few more, mostly old couples like us, with memories and traditions we'd spent a lifetime building and were not about to give up.

But it was the gaps I felt most keenly. The houses lost. The friends.

Marcia and Terry, from three doors up, who had started all this in so many ways. They were the first to lose someone to the Density. Their daughter, who had been young when Robert and I, newly married, had first moved in. She'd babysat Jason and Sue. Lovely girl. When the Density took her – to a one-bedroom flat in the inner-city, with too many stairs for her elderly parents to climb, and too busy a life for her to visit them – Terry and Robert had met in the local pub, and created this army over a couple of beers. They'd fought well, Marcia and Terry, and I could still taste the pavlova she'd bring to war council, if I tried.

We unfolded beach chairs and sat on the lawn, swatting at flies while Robert manned the BBQ, tongs glinting with fat and the sun.

'What we need,' Robert said, turning the snags, the bald spot on the back of his head reddening, 'is to take the fight to the Density itself.' He took a swig from his foam-wrapped beer. 'More than patrols and just cleaning-by-night. We need to drive it right outa here. Take back what was ours.'

He didn't look at me, when he said it, and I was grateful. Truth be told, I loved the lot of them for coming over, after what had happened the other night. For eating my food and not flinching when I passed them, limping.

This was what we fought for.

'How?' Dave asked, tomato sauce congealing in the thick grey whiskers on his chin.

Robert motioned with his head. 'Start with the park, move backwards. House by house if we have to.'

'If it was that easy, Rob, we'd have done it already.' Cheryl shook her head at him. 'Takes all we've got just to keep it at bay. It's too strong.'

Could I really blame them for their fear, their doubt? This was all that remained of a once-strong army, tied by friendship, by shared experience, by the vision Terry and Robert had given us. But all that remained now were neighbours, not friends, and none of them had been with us in those early days. Those first few tentative raids, when we found that even old and forgotten as we were, we could still fight back.

Robert bent over the snags again. 'We're not fighting with all we've got,' he said. 'Only what we've been willing to part with.'

The troops held their breath, wondering how far he would go.

'And that's all I can ask of you again: to give up what you feel is right. What will you risk to defend our homes, our street? Think hard, think long, because it will need to be strong enough to push back the Density. And know this: it has no such reservations. The Density will not hold anything back. So why should we?'

'You're asking us to give up everything, Rob, for a final push?' Cheryl cast a frown in my direction. I busied myself with the tomato sauce. 'You never asked us to do that before. No matter who fell in battle, or what houses the Density took.'

Robert was not fazed. 'I ask only what I have always asked, Cheryl. What this street itself has asked. For only what you are willing and able to give. That's what an old fashioned community does.'

We all knew what he was really asking, even if he couldn't bring himself to say it outright. That afternoon I pretended to doze over my cup of Lady Grey, and followed him into the bedroom when he tried to sneak away.

Caught him kneeling, awkwardly, reaching for the boxes beneath the bed.

'No, Bertie,' I whispered, but he heard me clear enough. 'Not this.'

'It's the only way, Alice.'

'I said no.'

He grunted, stood, held my shoulders in hands that were still so strong, though spotted now, and crooked in places. 'Don't expect me to stand back and watch the Density take you, love.'

'That was my mistake.' I held him. 'Don't you dare give yourself up because of it. Wouldn't be fair to live with that, all alone.'

'Love—'

'I said no.'

That evening, as we searched the back shed for stronger weaponry, I found a cluster of security doors and intercoms growing in a damp corner. Although baking soda and a good cloth got them off, I wondered what we really would have to sacrifice to dislodge a Density infestation as strong as this one.

'Wait for us, Alice.' Robert kissed me before pulling on his itchy balaclava.

Our guerrilla army carried powerful memories with them. Robert took the rusted old frames off the kids' bikes, the ones too ancient to ride but too dear to leave for collection on the kerb. Faded pink tassels still fluttered from Sue's handles, I remembered how bright they'd looked in the sun, as I held the back of her seat and helped her balance. There was a dent in Jason's, just above the front tyre, from when he fell and proved just how grown up he was by refusing to cry. I clutched hands at my chest to see them go into the darkness – the glint of an old steel bell the last thing I saw – and hoped those memories were enough.

Cheryl and Paul had decked themselves out in green, with cuttings from the Banksias in their yard attached to bike helmets that had been dipped in paint. They brought half a dozen dog leads clipped to collars still heavy with the names of long dead, much-loved pets. Robert pursed his lips at the sight of them, but I placed a hand on his shoulder before he could chide them.

'Dog leads?' he muttered to me. 'Is that how much they care about you?'

I squeezed, gently. 'If that is what they are willing to part with, then I will take it. And gladly.'

Dave kissed my cheek for luck. He smelled of beer and aftershave and carried the wicker chair his wife sat in, outside in the sun, during her final weeks. Robert nodded his silent approval and clapped the man on the back, earning a slightly drunken grin. I swallowed a sudden fear. Just how powerful was that chair? What would happen to Dave when its power ran out?

I was not involved in this assault. In this state, I would only slow them down. So I stood, broom at the ready, aproned and sturdy in the doorway while the rest crept across the road, commando-style, and into the building site. I left my post only once, to knock down a wall of lock-up letterboxes that tried to germinate on the front lawn.

Robert didn't stagger home with the dawn.

The complex growing across the street remained. Scarred, yes: parts of the building had withdrawn to the foundations like the tightening of wounded skin. And it was quiet, no drilling or hammering, none of the Density's noises. Just still. Injured, sleeping. Or simply waiting.

I remained on the front lawn, leaning on my broom. Jason's shirt had long since worn through. I'd replaced it with one of Sue's primary school skirts, pleated and maroon.

The street awoke around me with its usual, frantic rush. Most of them did not see the old woman standing alone in the middle of her lawn. They rarely did. Though a young boy, seven or so, waved at me as he was herded into the back seat of a fiercely blue vehicle, impractically low to the ground. And a young couple, house hunters perhaps, eyed me worriedly as they wandered past. But the rest were too caught in their constant movement, the forever-rush, to notice such shadows as myself.

By midday, I couldn't take it any longer. With Cheryl gone, the hydrangeas at the side of her house had been replaced by succulents and drought-resistant natives arranged into low-maintenance, drip-irrigated tiers. Difficult to look at. So I went inside, locked the door, and scrubbed the bathroom floor on hands and knees until I had cleared it of a spa bath big enough for two. I didn't cook any dinner, and sat in front of the tellie, not watching it, while I decided what to do.

The underground parking returned, this time a cobwebbing between the coffee table and rug. As I watched, hands twitching for my bleach, slate-grey bricks solidified and an unstable fluorescent light flickered up from below the house. I stood, pushed the table away. Stairs led down to whitewashed cement segmented into car-sized lots by strips of yellow paint.

Robert was down there, somewhere. I could feel him in my leg. Like he was just on the other side of those windows above my knee, knocking on the glass.

I hobbled to the bedroom. Leg stuck out at an ungainly angle, I crouched and, face pressed against jasmine smelling, fabric-softened sheets, felt the floorboards beneath the bed.

Our two most precious weapon caches. Robert's: an old briefcase, leather worn on the corners and locks missing their tiny keys. Mine: a shoebox of musty old cardboard, the black and white David Jones' houndstooth barely recognisable as faded grey.

I drew out my shoebox, wiped away a heavy layer of dust,

and opened the lid. Inside: a single black and white photograph of a small brick home surrounded by neatly clipped lawn, *all yours, love* written with long, excited loops in pencil on the back; a desiccated cicada shell, as fragile as spun glass; a small school notebook with yellowing pages and fading pencil; and a wedding invitation, once crisply white, names as bright gold as they ever were.

I sat back, for a moment, and ran my fingers over these, my oldest weapons. My most dear. While the Density surrounded us, while we fought with diluted drawings, rusty bikes, dog tags and shirts, it was these that ultimately kept us, and our homes, safe.

But if I used them up...

It would not do to dwell. Robert needed me.

So I took up my bottles and a handful of clean cloths. Two kinds of bleach for an assault like this: lemon-scented and the new mint fragrance. Still wasn't sure about that one. Bleach, to my senses, should always smell vaguely like a lemon grove going bad in the sun. An almost-full tub of Gumption, the really powerful stuff. I shoved them into the pockets of my apron, grabbed a large curly girl to be on the safe side, and my pre-made bicarb mixture.

Then I snapped on fresh rubber gloves, clutched my weapons to my chest, and descended into the carpark.

Cold wrapped around me, the too fresh, too crisp of air-conditioning and filters. The lounge room floor closed above my head.

Fluorescent lights flickered, jackhammering echoed, distant and constant. I followed it. The carpark stretched into a bleak forest of pillars, witches' hats, and still-wet paint. A lift chimed ahead, a large, red arrow snapping on, and its steel doors opened. Cheryl was slumped in the corner, her banksias gone, her helmet rolling loose near her feet.

I stumbled into as much of a run as I could manage. As the doors began to close, Cheryl lifted her head and I launched myself, arm outstretched, ignoring the plaster-crack somewhere in my foot, and triggered the doors just in time. I pushed my way inside and dropped hard to the linoleum floor.

'Alice?' Cheryl whispered, disbelieving and a little relieved. 'We— we weren't strong enough.' She swallowed so hard I could see the movement in her throat. 'Everything is so clean, so fresh. My house smells like wet dog, no matter what I do. Not like that in here.' She closed her eyes and tipped back her head as her right elbow sunk into the lift's mirrored wall. 'It smells like vanilla, in here. Not dog. Not dog at all.'

'No! Don't let it take you.' I pulled her arm out of the mirror, but she leaned away from me, drawing loud, long breaths in through her nose.

'You smell like bleach,' she whispered. 'Not vanilla either.'

I had no idea what else to do, so I slapped her, rattling bobby pins from her hair. Her eyes opened and she frowned.

'Steady on,' she said. Which made me smile.

'Where's Paul?'

'He was right beside me.' She lifted her hand, stared at her empty palm with consternation. 'He carried name tags. I've lost the leads.'

'Then we need to find him. And Robert. And the others.'

'Right. Yes. Yes, of course.'

Together, we stood. I needed her strength, couldn't put any weight at all on my dense leg. It had thickened so much it had torn the seams around my knee. A gas fitting for an outdoor BBQ protruded from my slacks. Cheryl, at least, was kind enough not to comment on it.

Worse was the stiffness that had moved up into my hip. I

tucked fingers in around my waistband and found a mosaic of glass tiles instead of skin. The Density in my leg was spreading.

'We need to hurry.'

The lift chimed, but no floor number lit up on the LCD display. The doors opened, our reflections – my arm around Cheryl, her hair a mess of grey curls tipped with stray green paint – wavered in the steel. We walked into the smell of chlorine and chalk. The fitness centre. The doors closed behind us, and we were plunged into darkness.

It was difficult to walk, even with her keeping me upright. But I managed to shuffle forward. Gradually, the smooth cement beneath our feet gave way to something loose, treacherous. Something like gravel, but larger, and damp. Slippery. I shuddered, thinking of digested material crunching beneath us: the stones of fallen houses, the branches of trees felled, and the bones of those who loved them. Everything the Density had devoured, and destroyed.

Something winked in the rough darkness, a tiny speck of weak light.

'What is that?' Cheryl choked over her words.

'Don't stop,' I hissed. 'Hold on to me.'

But she dragged me toward it. A single dog tag in the shape of a bone, the inscribed name almost illegible with age and rubbing. It held back the darkness like a candle flame, and the ground beneath it was fresh grass.

'Paul—' She tried to bend, to touch it, and I almost fell. One whole side of my body, foot to shoulder, had hardened to immobility.

'No!' I clutched at her. 'Don't let go. It will take you!'

As we watched, the dog tag was sucked down, into the ground, and the grass around it browned, flattened, and hardened into rock.

'So much for your weapons,' I whispered, and held mine even closer.

'Alice, oh Alice.'

Cheryl and I turned, while ice ran a course through me, and the darkness around us lifted enough, just enough, to see.

We had walked right past them.

Our army. Robert, buried to his waist in ruins and bones, face ashen and eyes imploring. Dave was... gone. Face down in splinters of wicker, body devoured flat. The others, the neighbours, were alive, though pale and buried to their heads. And Paul. Paul slumped, deflating, Paul gripping two remaining tags in one hand, the other clawing at rubble like he was trying to drag himself away.

'Run, Alice.' Robert sounded weak, his voice thin. 'We weren't strong enough to stop it, and I'm sorry. But you aren't Dense yet, not all of you. You can still run. Get as far away as you can. Don't let it take you.'

But I didn't do as my husband asked. Instead, I drew the mint-smelling bleach from my apron, unscrewed the lid, and dropped the cicada shell Jason had found into the noxious liquid. 'I've come to take you home.'

Robert's eyes widened. 'Alice, no—'

'Too late,' I said.

And the cicada dissolved. The memory of it remained for a moment, crisp in my mind, clear. Jason, just turned five years old, crying because he thought the insect was dead. He had children of his own now, and his oldest boy would be five in two months. Grandchildren I hardly ever saw. The Density owned them, tied them down with cables, images on bright screens, and security-guarded daycare.

Would they ever find anything as precious, delicate and heartbreaking, as Jason's cicada shell in their sterile lives?

Then the memory was gone, all of its presence, its power, infusing the bleach instead of me.

I bent, winced as glass shattered behind my knee, tipped bleach onto one of my clean cloths, and set to scrubbing. There was nothing I could do for Dave. So I kept my distance from his body, and worked on Paul instead.

The cicada was one of my most precious memories, and it was strong. But finite. I used up most of the bleach as I cleaned the Density from Paul's body. Mint scented fumes wreathed my head. Not right. Not right at all.

Then Paul lifted his head and Cheryl, desperate, snatched the cloth from my hand and freed him.

'Stop it, Alice. Stop it!' Robert struggled against the ruin and the rubble that held him, smacking down on it with bloodied fists and twisting his torso.

Smiling at him, I shuffled over to the neighbours. Pat first – her face was already white, cheeks sunken. 'But it's the only way.' It took all my bi-carb, and Sue's notebook, to free them. I tore each page, sprayed it with faintly bubbling water and scrubbed against the rubble until it dissolved in my hand. And with each page, the memory bled out of me like diluted watercolour. The summer we took the kids to a farm-stay holiday, and Sue discovered she loved horses. She worked in an office, now, bathed in fluorescent light and air-conditioning. She'd traded dust and horsehair for high heels and suits, and the Density.

The rubble withdrew in the face of her excitement, scribbled in 2B pencil and her first attempts at cursive. *Runny writing*. She'd been so proud.

Heavy iron scaffolding snaked its way across my shoulder blades.

Pat, Bill, and the bulk of our army, now freed, hovered behind me, uncertain what they should do.

'Take Dave,' I said. 'Get him out of here. It's the best we can do for him now.'

I could not stand, not any more. So I grasped the sawn-off edges of bricks, or protruding asbestos sheets, and dragged myself across the rubble. Towards Robert, still trapped and sinking slowly, no matter how hard he fought.

No one moved. Robert lifted his stricken face. 'Do it,' he said, voice rough, harsh. 'And hurry.'

That got them moving. Good soldiers always listened to their commander. Cheryl and Paul led the way, bleach-stinking cloth and dog tags held out before them. The neighbours carried Dave's desiccated body. Not the way Cheryl and I had come, but another I hoped led back to the park.

'Alice,' Robert whispered. 'Love. I'm sorry, love. I thought I could free you. From the leg, from the Density. I only wanted to keep things the way they were.'

I shook my head at him, drew out the Gumption, and the ancient photo in black and white. 'My own foolishness gave me this leg,' I said. 'I will not let you take the blame for that, Robert Anthony Hill.'

I shredded the photo, and dropped it into the thick white paste. Using the curly girl I swirled and swirled until the photo disappeared, then I started scrubbing.

The Density held Robert fast. It was strong. Maybe because he was the last of our army, and it was desperate to hold onto him. Or maybe because it already owned so much of me, and Robert and I were each a half of the other. Maybe the Density felt it had staked its claim on him.

But I had Gumption, a new curly girl – not yet tangled, rusted, or mottled with bits of dried food – and a good set of dishwashing gloves. And my memories of home.

Robert ran a hand through my hair as I worked – it was

about all he could do. Used to be thick, that hair, and dark. I hoped he would remember me like that.

'I was enjoying this, Alice,' he said.

I looked up just long enough to lift my eyebrows in a question. It was hard work, all this cleaning, and hot. If I could still feel my back, and knees, they would be aching by now.

'All of it. Patrolling, keeping that bloody Density back where it belonged.' He chuckled. 'Even Paul and Cheryl and their ridiculous camouflage.'

'But we did this because we had to,' I said, as I scraped away the rubble around his right leg, revealing grass and damp, fresh-smelling dirt. Wouldn't take long before it returned. I had to work quickly. 'To keep some of this place the way it used to be.'

Robert was looking away from me, into the darkness and the distance of the foundations. 'Kids have grown up, we've gotten old, and this street changes all around us. That's normal, love. That's life. No, I want to keep doing *this*. Fighting for something good, fighting in secret, being someone more than the bloke who goes to work and comes home then goes to work again the next day. Even thought I could retire, if I still had a fight to fight.'

Robert, retire? Perhaps it was the Density talking.

'But I've buggered it up, haven't I? I let your leg happen, and now Dave. It's all my fault, love. It was war. I should have understood what that meant.'

'No.' I scraped the bottom of the plastic tub, and scoured the last of the rubble away. 'It wasn't—'

But it was hard to talk now. A network of pipes grew rampant along the right side of my body. They welded themselves to the rubble, burrowed in search of a sewerage system.

I dropped the empty container, the curly girl fell to filings in my hand.

But Robert, at least, could pull himself free. He shook dirt from his clothes, and drew dinted, rusted, tarnished handlebars from his jacket. All that remained of his failed weaponry.

'Go—' I tried to speak. 'Hurry.'

Instead, he took hold of the decorative lattice that was my elbow and started pulling. But my foundations – pipes and wires and steel and cement – ran deep, and I did not budge.

Finally, he wrapped his arms around me, awkwardly, and held me. I could barely feel him, hardly move. He smelled of charred onions and sausage fat.

'Take—' I struggled. 'Please—'

He looked down to my apron, pulled tight and strangely shaped across my terracotta facade and the patterns in my brickwork. The lemon-scented bleach, and an invitation to our wedding.

'Bleach, love?' He whispered, throat thick, voice choked. But he did as he knew I was asking. And he tore up the invitation, and he shoved it into the bleach bottle, and he shook it until the cardboard dissolved, and with it, the last of my weapons. My memories. The past I held on to, so tightly.

At least it was the lemon one.

Even as my memories of him started to fade, Robert brandished his handlebars and the bleach bottle and he ran. Roaring anger, roaring tears, splashing toxic-smelling liquid before him, around him, he escaped.

And together, the Density and I forgot him.

I stood in the front yard, clutching her broom, and watched as she drove to work in the morning. Not my Alice, not any more. She'd never cake her face with makeup like that, or use bleach in her hair – bleach was a weapon, it belonged on a cloth – and she'd never drive something as useless as a red car with two seats and no bloody roof. I'd wrapped the broom in her blue floral dress, the one she'd said was for young things, not old women, but I would not let her throw out. Still remembered the soft touch of its fabric – silk and something, I thought – the way it clung to her waist and swung round her thighs. She'd laugh when I held her and I could feel it through her whole body; joy, travelling as warmth through my palms.

So for all the Density had changed her, I still knew her. And I watched the scraps of her it left for me, every morning.

She didn't see me. And I felt like I really was fading into nothing, becoming less than memory, when she turned out of the hulking garage across the street and her eyes skimmed right through me. I did not exist.

The Density had reduced us to an army of three. After Dave's death, and Alice's sacrifice, only Cheryl and Paul stuck it out. Never thought they did it for the right reasons, but then, neither did I. You take what troops you can. They liked the drama of it. The camouflage and the scuttling low, under cover of darkness, wielding petty trinkets against a much greater foe. Doomed, but enjoying the ride.

I wasn't sure I could do that any more.

I took my weapons cache out from under the bed, once Alice left. Rested each fine and precious memory on the doona cover. It wouldn't take much, the Density across the road was strong. A sturdy broom, a handful of sandpaper, maybe even some of Alice's hoard of lemon-scented bleach, and my memories. All of them. It would be enough, surely, to force my way through the garage and the courtyard and the gym and whatever else the Density thrust into my way. And if I found her apartment, studio, whatever it was they call it these days, and if I stood there while my memories dissolved, if I gave myself to the Density then maybe... maybe it would let me stay. With her. With what's left of her.

But I didn't think Alice, if she remembered me, if she could even see me, would like that. Not after what she had done. So even though I wasn't sure which was braver – giving myself up, like she did, or sticking to our futile war – I left my memories on the bed, took up her broom instead, and waited for the evening assault.

Credits

Some of the pieces appearing in this collection were first published elsewhere; permissions and copyright information as follows:

- Preface Copyright © 2021 Joanne Anderton
- "The Sea At Night" © 2011. First appeared in *Red Dead Heart*, edited by Russell B. Farr (Ticonderoga Publications)
- "Cold Beneath the Bougainvillea" © 2008. First appeared in *Black Box*, edited by Shane Jiraiya Cummings (Brimstone Press)
- "Simulation Theory" © 2014. Fist appeared in COSMOS Magazine Feb/Mar 2014.
- "Thread Embrace" © 2007. First appeared in *The Harrow, Vol 10, No 8*, edited by Dru Pagliassotti
- "Mirror Dirt" © 2007. First appeared in *Flashspec Volume Two*, edited by Neil Cladingboel (Equilibrium Books)
- "Little Ghost Boy" © 2009. First appeared in

Midnight Echo #3, edited by Stephen Studach (AHWA)

- "High Density" © 2012. First Appeared in *Andromeda Spaceways Inflight Magazine #53*

Joanne Anderton is an Australia author of speculative fiction, creative non-fiction, and children's books, who until recently was living and working in rural Japan. Her speculative fiction includes the novels in the *Veiled Worlds* series – *Debris*, *Suited* and *Guardian* – and the short story collection *The Bone Chime Song and Other Stories*. She has won multiple awards for her speculative fiction, including the Australian Shadows Award, Ditmar and Aurealis Awards. Her short fiction has been reprinted in several *Year's Best* anthologies, and she's received international review coverage in *The New York Journal of Books*, *The Guardian*, *Library Journal* and *Publishers Weekly*.

Her children's picture book *The Flying Optometrist*, was published by the National Library of Australia and was a

CBCA notable book. Her non-fiction has been published in *Island Magazine, Meanjin* and *The Japan News*.

Joanne has a Masters of Arts in Creative Writing, and worked for many years in book publishing, marketing and distribution. She is currently undertaking a PhD in Creative Writing at The University of Queensland.

Find her online at JoanneAnderton.com

facebook.com/JoanneAndertonAuthor
twitter.com/joanneanderton
amazon.com/Joanne-Anderton/e/B00K1B0YTK

Thank You For Buying This Brain Jar Press
Chapbook

To receive special offers, bonus content, and info on
new releases and other great reads, visit us
online at www.BrainJarPress.com